P9-DYZ-147
DISNEY
BEAUTY
AND THE
BEAST
BELLE'S
TALE
TOKYOPOP®

# Contents

Dear Readers:

Welcome to a very special project: the twin companion *BEAUTY AND THE BEAST* manga set! This particular manga is *BELLE'S TALE*, where we relive the story from Belle's perspective.

While our talented Japanese artists iterated and iterated to embody the Beast's ferocious yet sensitive nature, our artists focused on intricate details and nuances when illustrating Belle. Working closely with the Disney team, the artists evolved the perfect balance of shojo manga and classic Belle. Be sure to study the Concept Art section found in the back of the book to experience this artistic evolution.

Certainly, the locations and set pieces from the film are reflected in this manga through careful recreations. Notice the detail you'll find in the Villeneuve prison scene, or Belle's bed in the Beast's castle. Every angle needed to be anticipated by the artists since there are no cameras to record such images. In some cases where the film references were not always available, the artists had to rely on their imaginations and highly disciplined fingers.

And with no songs emanating from each page of the book, Belle's inner thoughts are expressed by traditional shojo manga monologue. We recommend playing the movie soundtrack - or even humming it quietly! - while reading Belle's diary-like comments.

So, join Belle on her journey finding her inner strength and embracing the possibilities of a life pursuing one's dreams.

TOKYOPOP is proud to bring you *BELLE'S TALE*!!

--- Team TOKYOPOP

びゅーてぃーあんど
びーすと

Disney
BEAUTY
AND THE
BEAST

ONCE UPON A TIME, IN THE BEAUTIFUL CITY OF PARIS...
CHAPTER 1
A LITTLE GIRL WAS BORN TO TWO LOVING PARENTS.

ALTHOUGH THEY HAD
VERY LITTLE WEALTH...
...THEY HAD
EVERYTHING THEIR
HEARTS DESIRED.

THEY FILLED THEIR LITTLE HOUSE WITH LOVE...
AND THEY LIVED HAPPILY EVER AFTER...

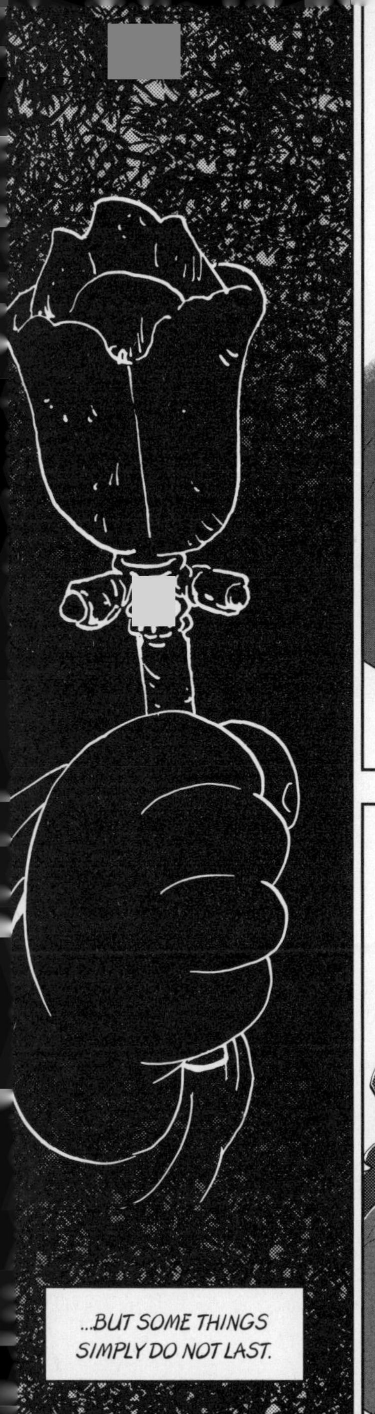
...BUT SOME THINGS SIMPLY DO NOT LAST.

THE LITTLE GIRL NEVER FOUND OUT WHAT HAPPENED TO HER MOTHER...
...AND HER FATHER NEVER SPOKE OF IT.
AND SO ANOTHER STORY BEGINS...
...OR IS IT MERELY A RETELLING OF THE SAME ONE?

DAY AFTER DAY,
ALWAYS THE SAME...
I FEEL LIKE I HAVE AN
EXCITING NEW BOOK
TO READ...
...BUT I JUST CAN'T GET
PAST THE PROLOGUE.
AM I THE ONLY ONE IN
THIS ENTIRE TOWN WHO
WANTS TO EXPERIENCE
NEW THINGS?

GOOD MORNING, BELLE. WHERE DID YOU RUN OFF TO THIS WEEK?
TWO CITIES IN NORTHERN ITALY!
THE CASTLES, THE ART... THERE WAS EVEN A MASQUERADE BALL!
HAVE YOU GOT ANY NEW PLACES TO GO?
I'M AFRAID NOT. BUT YOU MAY REREAD ANY OF THE OLD ONES YOU'D LIKE.
THANK YOU, PÈRE ROBERT.
YOUR LIBRARY MAKES OUR SMALL CORNER OF THE WORLD ALMOST FEEL BIG.

That girl is so strange.
Look, there she goes...
No wonder her name means 'beauty.'
Very different from the rest of us.
But I'm afraid she's rather odd.
I CAN HEAR THEM TALKING ABOUT ME...
THEY THINK I DON'T NOTICE, BUT I DO.

GOOD MORNING, BELLE.
WONDERFUL BOOK YOU HAVE THERE!
YOU'VE READ IT?
WELL NOT THAT ONE. BUT YOU KNOW. BOOKS.

FOR YOUR DINNER TABLE.
SHALL I JOIN YOU TONIGHT?
SORRY, NOT TONIGHT.
BUSY?
NO...

I'VE NEVER UNDERSTOOD HOW HE'S MANAGED TO FOOL EVERYONE IN THE VILLAGE.
MM,
HE MAKES ME FEEL...QUEASY.
OH, GOOD, BELLE, YOU'RE BACK.
WHERE WERE YOU?

FIRST I WENT TO ST. PETERSBURG TO SEE THE TSAR,
THEN I WENT FISHING IN THE BOTTOM OF THE WELL–
HMM, YES, SOUNDS FUN.
CAN YOU PLEASE HAND ME THE–
DO YOU THINK I'M ... ODD?
PAPA?

WHERE DID YOU GET AN IDEA LIKE THAT?
OH, I DON'T KNOW. PEOPLE TALK...
THERE ARE WORSE THINGS THAN BEING TALKED ABOUT.

THIS VILLAGE MAY BE SMALL-MINDED,
BUT IT'S ALSO SAFE.
I THINK YOUR MOTHER WOULD HAVE HOPED YOU STAY SAFE.
TELL ME MORE ABOUT HER?
カチャ
カチャ
TO KNOW ANYTHING MORE, YOU JUST HAVE TO LOOK IN THE MIRROR.

YOUR MOTHER WAS FEARLESS.

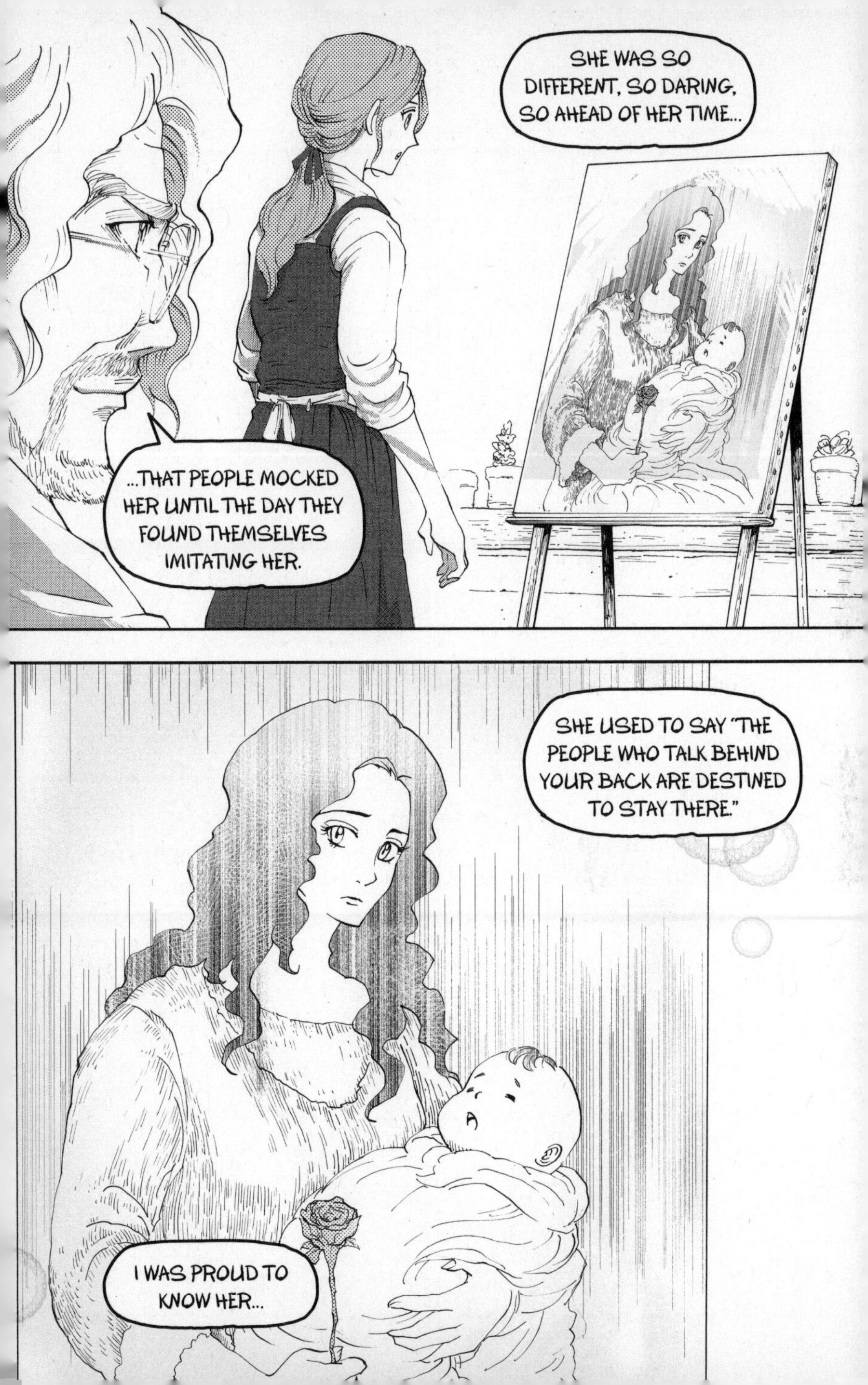
SHE WAS SO DIFFERENT, SO DARING, SO AHEAD OF HER TIME...
...THAT PEOPLE MOCKED HER UNTIL THE DAY THEY FOUND THEMSELVES IMITATING HER.
SHE USED TO SAY "THE PEOPLE WHO TALK BEHIND YOUR BACK ARE DESTINED TO STAY THERE."
I WAS PROUD TO KNOW HER...

IT'S BEAUTIFUL
IT'S STILL NOT RIGHT.
YOU WON'T EVER THINK IT'S RIGHT, PAPA...
I THINK SHE WOULD HAVE LOVED IT.

NOW IF YOU GO OUT AT ALL, MAKE SURE YOU'RE HOME BEFORE DARK.
STOP WORRYING, PAPA.
WHAT WOULD YOU LIKE ME TO BRING YOU FROM THE MARKET?
A ROSE LIKE THE ONE IN THE PAINTING.
YOU ASK FOR THAT EVERY YEAR.
AND EVERY YEAR, YOU BRING IT.

THE... B....LUE BIRD
FL-FL...IES...
GOOD!

ザッ
WHAT ARE YOU DOING?
HEADMASTER...
GIRLS DON'T READ!
AND WHAT IS THIS?
チラ

NOW, BELLE, THE WASHING IS SUPPOSED TO BE DONE BY HAND.
TO MAKE CERTAIN IT GETS DONE WELL, AND SO YOUNG PEOPLE LIKE YOU CAN LEARN THE VALUE OF HARD WORK.
WHAT ABOUT LEARNING THE VALUE OF INGENUITY?
DON'T TRY TO CONFUSE ME WITH FOREIGN WORDS, YOUNG LADY.

YOU'RE THE HEADMASTER!
FOREIGN--?!
THAT GIRL IS SUCH A TROUBLEMAKER!
WHAT IS THAT CONTRAPTION?
THAT'S NOT HOW YOU DO LAUNDRY...
NOW, HOLD ON!
Troublemaker!
Boooo!
Boooo!

パァン!!
THIS IS NOT HOW GOOD PEOPLE BEHAVE!

EVERYONE, GO HOME. NOW!
I'M NOT SURE WHAT'S GOING ON HERE,
BUT I'M PRETTY SURE I JUST FIXED IT.

I WAS PRETTY GREAT BACK THERE, WASN'T I?
LIKE BEING BACK IN COMMAND DURING THE WAR...
WE'RE BOTH FIGHTERS. BUT CAN I GIVE YOU A LITTLE ADVICE ABOUT THE VILLAGERS?
THEY'RE NEVER GOING TO TRUST THE KIND OF CHANGE WE'RE TRYING TO BRING.

I KNOW MY FATHER WANTS TO KEEP ME SAFE...
ALL I WANTED WAS TO TEACH A CHILD TO READ...
...AND I UNDERSTAND WHY, BUT...
BELLE, I'M SURE YOU THINK I HAVE IT ALL.
BUT THERE IS SOMETHING I'M MISSING...
A WIFE.
GASTON...

THANK YOU FOR TAKING ME HOME.
BUT I WILL NEVER MARRY YOU.
OH...!
WH... WHAT?!

I WANT TO CHANGE THE WORLD FOR THE BETTER.

CHAPTER 2
I MISS PAPA WHEN HE GOES AWAY...
...BUT I ALWAYS LOVED HAVING THIS LITTLE HOUSE TO MYSELF.
IT'S NICE TO HAVE A PLACE THAT'S JUST MINE...

PHILIPPE? YOU'RE BACK HERE ALONE?
WHERE'S PAPA?
OH, NO...
...PAPA!
HURRY, PHILIPPE!
LEAD ME TO HIM!
...I JUST HAVE TO FIND HIM...!
HE PROBABLY HASN'T BEEN OUT HERE VERY LONG.
ダダダ...
!!
WAIT...! IS THAT A TOWER...?
ギュッ

HELLO...?
コツ
コツ...

PAPA...?!
PAPA?!
BELLE...?
BELLE, YOU MUST LEAVE THIS PLACE!
BELLE, THIS CASTLE IS ALIVE! YOU MUST GET AWAY BEFORE HE FINDS YOU!
WE'VE GOT TO GET YOU HOME!

WHO ARE YOU?
I'VE COME FOR MY FATHER. RELEASE HIM!
YOUR FATHER IS A THIEF.
LIAR!

HE STOLE A ROSE!

THE ROSE WAS FOR ME...!
PUNISH ME, NOT HIM.
NO! HE SAID I WAS HIS PRISONER FOREVER.
A LIFE'S SENTENCE FOR A ROSE?

ギュッ!!
I RECEIVED ETERNAL DAMNATION FOR ONE— I'M MERELY LOCKING HIM AWAY.
ETERNAL DAMNATION...?
NOW... DO YOU TRULY WISH TO TAKE YOUR FATHER'S PLACE?
COME INTO THE LIGHT.
A LIFE'S SENTENCE...
MY POOR FATHER HAS ALREADY BEEN THROUGH TOO MUCH.
AT LEAST IF IT'S ME, I HAVE A CHANCE OF ESCAPING...

WHAT IS HE...?!

CHOOSE!
BUT YOU'LL DIE HERE!
BELLE, I WON'T LET YOU DO THIS!
NO, BELLE... I COULDN'T SAVE YOUR MOTHER,
BUT I CAN SAVE YOU. NOW GO!
PAPA, I HAVE TO DO THIS...

I WILL LEAVE.
OPEN THE DOOR. I NEED A MINUTE ALONE WITH HIM.
WHEN THIS DOOR CLOSES, IT WILL NOT OPEN AGAIN!
PHEW...

NO, THIS WAS MY FAULT. NOW LISTEN, BELLE...
I'M SORRY, PAPA, I SHOULD HAVE GONE WITH YOU...
FORGET ABOUT ME, I'VE HAD MY LIFE...
FORGET YOU? EVERYTHING I AM IS BECAUSE OF YOU...!
I LOVE YOU, PAPA...
I'M NOT AFRAID. AND I PROMISE... I WILL ESCAPE.

YOU TOOK HIS PLACE—WHY?
HE IS MY FATHER.

PAPA...
I PROMISE...
ギュッ
I'LL SEE YOU AGAIN.

# CHAPTER 3

カッ…
コッ…
コッ…
FORGIVE MY INTRUSION, MADEMOISELLE...
...BUT THE MASTER HAS SENT ME TO ESCORT YOU TO YOUR ROOM.
!?

MY ROOM? BUT I THOUGHT...
YOU THOUGHT WRONG.
HE IS A BEAST, NOT A MONSTER.
'ALLO.

WHAT ARE YOU?
I AM LUMIERE.
AND YOU CAN TALK...
OF COURSE HE CAN.
AS HEAD OF THE HOUSEHOLD, I DEMAND TO KNOW WHAT YOU ARE DOING.

READY, MISS?
PAPA SAID THIS CASTLE WAS ALIVE, BUT...
...I CERTAINLY DIDN'T EXPECT THIS!
WHAT DOES THAT MEAN?!
IT IS BETTER TO ASK FOR FORGIVENESS THAN PERMISSION.
YOU MUST FORGIVE OUR FIRST IMPRESSIONS. I HOPE YOU WERE NOT TOO STARTLED!
STARTLED? WHY WOULD I BE STARTLED? I'M TALKING TO A CANDLE.
CANDEL-A-BRA. PLEASE. ENORMOUS DIFFERENCE.
BUT WE DO HOPE YOU ENJOY YOUR STAY HERE. THE CASTLE IS YOUR HOME NOW, SO FEEL FREE TO GO ANYWHERE...
--EXCEPT THE WEST WING!
WHY, WHAT'S IN THE WEST WING?
UH, NOTHING... THIS WAY, PLEASE!

WELCOME TO YOUR NEW HOME.
IT'S BEAUTIFUL!
OF COURSE! MASTER WANTED YOU TO HAVE THE FINEST ROOM IN THE CASTLE.

WELL, ALL RIGHT.
OH DEAR! WE WEREN'T EXPECTING GUESTS.
ぼふん
!
ENCHANTE, MADEMOISELLE!
AH, HELLO...

ぐおお———…
My wardrobe is snoring.
DO NOT BE ALARMED, MADEMOISELLE! THIS IS JUST YOUR WARDROBE.
MEET MADAME DE GARDEROBE. A GREAT SINGER.
A better sleeper.
FINALLY! A WOMAN!
MADAME, WE HAVE SOMEONE FOR YOU TO DRESS.
I WILL FIND YOU SOMETHING WORTHY OF A PRINCESS.
BUT I'M NOT A PRINCESS

COME HERE, FROUFROU!
ワン ワン!
COME BACK HERE, YOU OVER-UPHOLSTERED...!
ANYWAY... IF YOU HAVE FURTHER NEEDS, THE STAFF WILL ATTEND TO THEM.
WE ARE AT YOUR SERVICE. AU REVOIR!

HOW DID YOU ALL GET HERE?
WELL.. ALL IT TAKES IS A STORMY NIGHT AND ONE SPOILED LITTLE PRINCE...
ぴ,
ぐ——…
ヒラ…
!

キュッ
NOT QUITE LONG ENOUGH...
コン
コン

ぐい…
JUST A MINUTE!
ギュッ ギュッ!!
YOU WILL JOIN ME FOR DINNER!
I DON'T KNOW WHAT TO DO, BUT I KNOW I DON'T WANT TO HAVE DINNER WITH HIM!
YOU'VE TAKEN ME PRISONER AND NOW YOU'RE ASKING ME TO DINE WITH YOU?
ARE YOU MAD?
IT WOULD GIVE ME GREAT PLEASURE IF YOU WOULD JOIN ME FOR DINNER...

IT WOULD GIVE ME GREAT PLEASURE...
...IF YOU WOULD GO AWAY.
AND I TOLD YOU NO!
I TOLD YOU TO COME TO DINNER!
I'D STARVE BEFORE I EVER ATE A MEAL WITH YOU!
BE MY GUEST. GO AHEAD AND STARVE!
HOW DARE HE...?!

WHAT'S GOING ON?!
HE ASKED ME TO DINE WITH HIM!
CAN YOU BELIEVE IT?! AFTER HE CALLED MY FATHER A THIEF, FORCED ME TO CHOOS HIS LIFE OR MINE–
I KNOW WHAT IT LOOKS LIKE, DEAR, BUT THE MASTER ISN'T SO BAD, ONCE YOU GET TO KNOW HIM...
I DON'T WANT TO GET TO KNOW HIM!

グッ
グッ
コン
コンッ
I TOLD YOU TO GO AWAY!
DON'T WORRY, DEAR, IT'S NOT THE MASTER.
IT'S MRS. POTTS!

IT'S A VERY LONG JOURNEY, MY LAMB....
MADAME! WAKE UP!
LET ME FIX YOU UP BEFORE YOU GO.
カタ...
I HAVE FOUND, IN MY EXPERIENCE, THAT MOST TROUBLES SEEM LESS TROUBLING AFTER A BRACING CUP OF TEA.

BUT WHAT HAPPENED HERE? IS THIS AN ENCHANTMENT? A CURSE?
SLOWLY, NOW, CHIP. DON'T SPILL THE TEA. OR SECRETS.
SHE GUESSED IT, MAMA. SHE'S SMART.
SECRETS...?

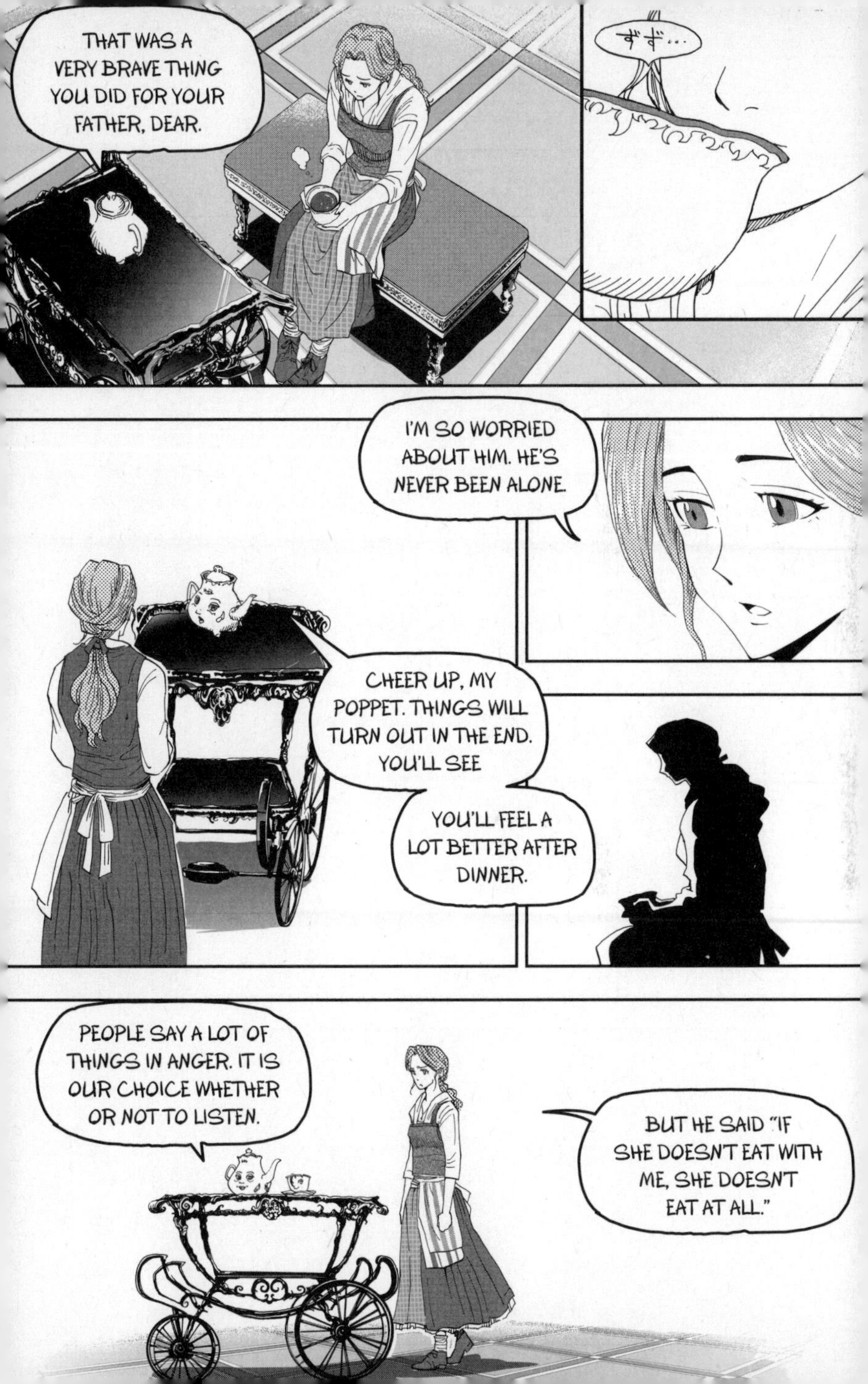
THAT WAS A VERY BRAVE THING YOU DID FOR YOUR FATHER, DEAR.
ずず…
I'M SO WORRIED ABOUT HIM. HE'S NEVER BEEN ALONE.
CHEER UP, MY POPPET. THINGS WILL TURN OUT IN THE END. YOU'LL SEE
YOU'LL FEEL A LOT BETTER AFTER DINNER.
PEOPLE SAY A LOT OF THINGS IN ANGER. IT IS OUR CHOICE WHETHER OR NOT TO LISTEN.
BUT HE SAID "IF SHE DOESN'T EAT WITH ME, SHE DOESN'T EAT AT ALL."

I THOUGHT WE WERE HAVING DINNER...

THEY'RE ALL SO KIND, SO EAGER TO PLEASE...
ARE THEY OBJECTS COME TO LIFE...
...OR WERE THEY ONCE PEOPLE?
CAN I HELP THEM SOMEHOW?
I ONLY CAME HERE TO FIND MY FATHER, BUT I'VE FOUND MORE THAN I EVER EXPECTED TO.

CHAPTER 4
THAT WAS WONDERFUL, THANK YOU.
IT WAS OUR PLEASURE, DEAR.
I DON'T UNDERSTAND WHY YOU'RE ALL BEING SO KIND TO ME...
YOU DESERVE NOTHING LESS, MY LOVE.
BUT YOU'RE AS TRAPPED HERE AS I AM. DON'T YOU EVER WANT TO ESCAPE?
THE MASTER'S NOT AS TERRIBLE AS HE APPEARS.
SOMEWHERE DEEP IN HIS SOUL, THERE'S A PRINCE OF A FELLOW... JUST WAITING TO BE SET FREE.

LUMIERE MENTIONED SOMETHING ABOUT THE WEST WING...
OH, NEVER YOU MIND ABOUT THAT!
NOW OFF TO BED.
CAN I GET YOU ANYTHING FOR YOUR ROOM, DEARIE?
NO, YOU'VE ALREADY DONE SO MUCH.
THANK YOU. GOOD NIGHT.
NIGHT-NIGHT.
I WONDER WHY THEY DIDN'T WANT ME TO KNOW ABOUT THIS PLACE...

THIS MAKES ME NERVOUS BUT I CAN'T RESIST...
...I'M IN AN ENCHANTED CASTLE AFTER ALL!

!?
GASP

WHO...?

SHE LOOKS SO CALM.
BUT ALSO, MAYBE... SAD?
A ROSE...?
HE SAID SOMETHING ABOUT ETERNAL DAMNATION FOR A ROSE...

IT'S JUST... FLOATING.
HOW...?
NO--!

!
WHAT ARE YOU DOING HERE?
WHAT DID YOU DO TO IT?!

NOTHING...
DO YOU REALIZE WHAT YOU COULD HAVE DONE?!
YOU COULD HAVE DAMNED US ALL!
GET OUT!

I CAN'T TAKE THIS ANYMORE!
I DON'T CARE HOW MUCH THEY SAY HE ISN'T A MONSTER...
...HE STILL ACTS LIKE ONE.
EVERYONE ELSE IS NICE, BUT...
MADEMOISELLE! WHAT ARE YOU DOING?
GETTING OUT OF HERE!
...I WON'T STAY. NOT WITH HIM!
YOU DON'T WANT TO GO OUT THERE, DEAR!
!

DID HE COME AFTER ME?
I THINK I MADE IT...

THE WAY HE LOOKED AT ME AS WE STOOD THERE...
...I'VE NEVER SEEN THAT EXPRESSION BEFORE.
ALL I HAVE SEEN IS ANGER... FRUSTRATION, STUBBORNNESS...
BUT WHEN HE LOOKED AT ME AFTER THE WOLVES FLED...
HE LOOKED SAD...
...HE LOOKED LOST.
YOU HAVE TO STAND...
YOU HAVE TO HELP ME...

IF YOU HELD STILL, IT WOULDN'T HURT AS MUCH.
チャプ
IF YOU HADN'T RUN AWAY, THIS WOULDN'T HAVE HAPPENED.
IF YOU HADN'T FRIGHTENED ME, I WOULDN'T HAVE RUN AWAY!
WELL, YOU SHOULD LEARN TO CONTROL YOUR TEMPER!
WELL, YOU SHOULDN'T HAVE BEEN UP HERE!
THIS IS WORSE THAN I THOUGHT...

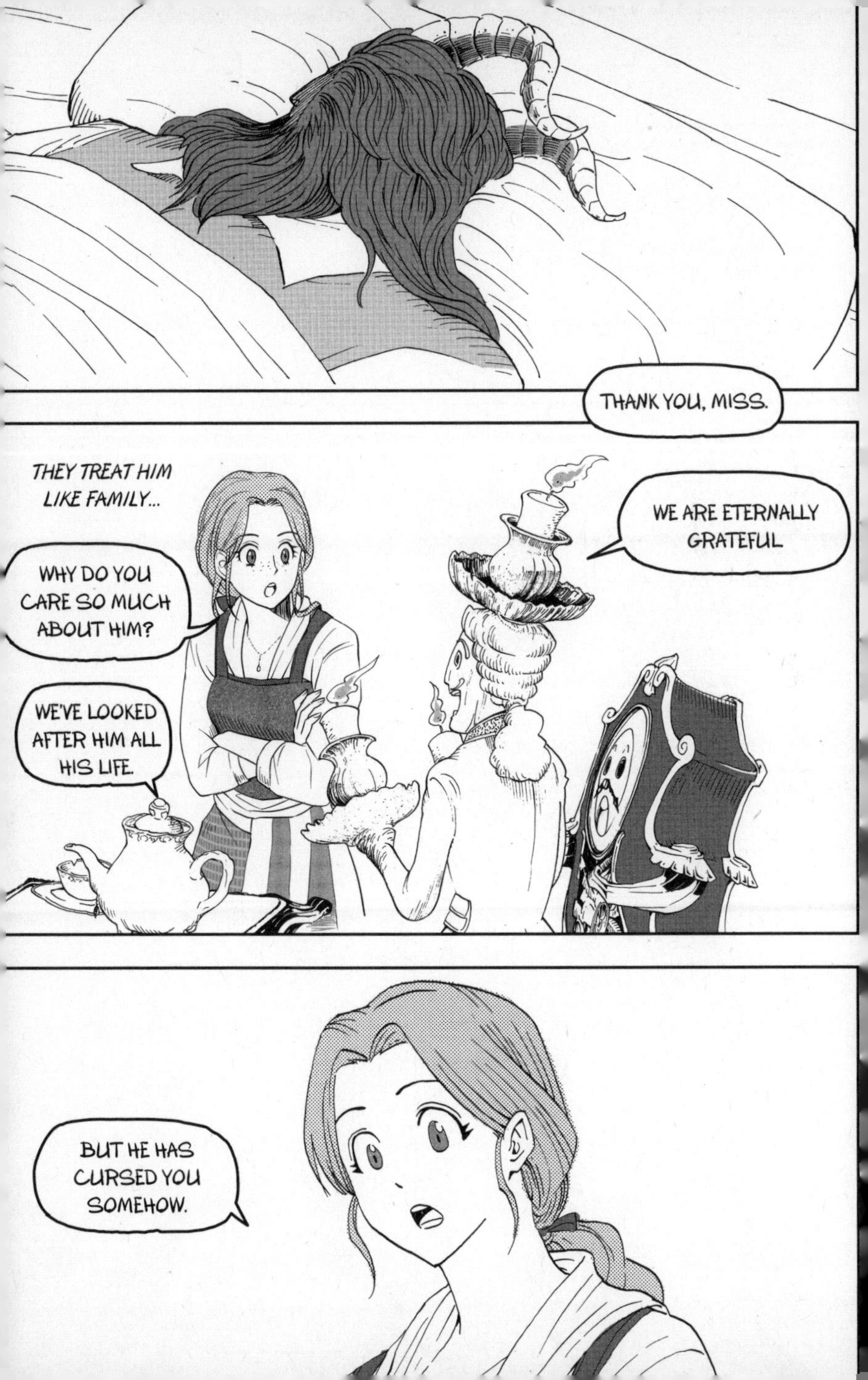
THANK YOU, MISS.
THEY TREAT HIM LIKE FAMILY...
WHY DO YOU CARE SO MUCH ABOUT HIM?
WE'VE LOOKED AFTER HIM ALL HIS LIFE.
WE ARE ETERNALLY GRATEFUL
BUT HE HAS CURSED YOU SOMEHOW.

YOU'RE QUITE RIGHT THERE, DEAR.
YOU SEE, WHEN THE MASTER LOST HIS MOTHER...
HIS CRUEL FATHER TOOK THAT SWEET, INNOCENT LAD...
AND TWISTED HIM UP TO BE JUST LIKE HIM...
I SEE...
...WE DID NOTHING.

IT DOESN'T EXCUSE HIS BEHAVIOR... BUT...
...IF THAT WERE ME...

...I THINK I WOULD BE PRETTY ANGRY, TOO.
I THINK, IF I HADN'T BEEN RAISED WITH LOVE...

...IT MIGHT BE HARDER FOR ME TO RECOGNIZE IT.
THIS ROOM DOESN'T LOOK SO SCARY IN THE SUNLIGHT...

す…
WHAT HAPPENS WHEN THE LAST PETAL FALLS?
THE MASTER REMAINS A BEAST FOREVER.
AND THE REST OF US BECOME RUBBISH.
I WANT TO HELP YOU.
THERE MUST BE SOME WAY TO LIFT THE CURSE!

WELL, THERE IS ONE—
ギィイイ…
IT'S NOT FOR YOU TO WORRY ABOUT, LAMB.
WE'VE MADE OUR BED AND WE MUST LIE IN IT.
ギュッ!!
I DON'T THINK ANYONE WOULD STOP ME IF I TRIED TO LEAVE NOW, BUT...
MAYBE, IF I STAY...
I CAN FIND SOME WAY TO HELP...

"LOVE CAN TRANSPOSE TO FORM AND DIGNITY..."
CHAPTER 5
"LOVE LOOKS NOT WITH THE EYES, BUT WITH THE MIND..."
"AND THEREFORE—"
"AND THEREFORE IS WINGED CUPID PAINTED BLIND."
AND THEREFORE IS WINGED CUPID PAINTED BLIND.

SO YOU KNOW SHAKESPEARE.
I HAD AN EXPENSIVE EDUCATION.
ACTUALLY, *ROMEO AND JULIET* IS MY FAVORITE PLAY.

ALL THAT HEARTACHE AND PINING AND--
THERE ARE SO MANY BETTER THINGS TO READ.
LIKE WHAT?
FOLLOW ME.

THIS IS AMAZING...
IT'S WONDERFUL.
I'VE NEVER SEEN SO MANY BOOKS IN MY LIFE...!
YOU THINK SO?
THEN, IT'S YOURS.

MY HEART IS POUNDING.

I WONDER IF SOMETHING CHANGED...

...OR IF THIS SIDE OF HIM WAS ALWAYS THERE.

HE WAS SO RUDE AND INTIMIDATING BEFORE,
BUT NOW THERE'S SOMETHING ELSE...

I SEE SWEETNESS AND KINDNESS IN HIM
NOW, BUT ALSO, PERHAPS, FEAR...?

WHAT COULD SOMETHING AS FEARSOME AS A BEAST EVER BE AFRAID OF?
AND WHEN HE'S NOT AFRAID OR UPSET...HE'S SO GENTLE AND UNCERTAIN.

THOUGH I WAS CERTAINLY FRIGHTENED OF HIM, HIS TEMPER HAS CALMED...
HE ASKS INSTEAD OF DEMANDING. HE APOLOGIZES AND LEARNS.

I FEEL AS THOUGH I SEE WHO HE TRULY IS.
HE LOOKS SO... PEACEFUL.
GUINEVERE AND LANCELOT.
BELLE?!
UH... IT'S ABOUT KING ARTHUR AND THE ROUND TABLE. SWORDS, FIGHTING...
BUT STILL.. IT'S A ROMANCE.

FELT LIKE A CHANGE.
くす…
ER... I NEVER THANKED YOU FOR SAVING MY LIFE.
I NEVER THANKED YOU FOR NOT LEAVING ME TO DIE.
MY HEART IS SKIPPING... IT FEELS LIKE CHASING BUTTERFLIES IN SPRING.

HA, DO IT AGAIN!
ボン
ボン
ガッ!!
BE CAREFUL LUMIERE!
WELL... THEY KNOW HOW TO HAVE A GOOD TIME.
SOMETIMES WHEN I TAKE MY DINNER, I LISTEN TO THEIR LAUGHTER...
...AND PRETEND I AM EATING WITH THEM.

YOU SHOULD. THEY'D LOVE THAT.
I'VE TRIED...
WHEN I ENTER THE ROOM, THE LAUGHTER DIES.
I KNOW WHAT THAT FEELS LIKE.
ME, TOO.
OR SOMETIMES WORSE..... SOMETIMES, WHEN I ENTER A ROOM, THE LAUGHTER BEGINS.

READ THIS WAY
THE VILLAGERS SAY THAT I'M A "FUNNY GIRL," BUT...
...I DON'T THINK THEY MEAN IT AS A COMPLIMENT.
I'M SORRY, YOUR VILLAGE SOUNDS TERRIBLE.
IT WASN'T TERRIBLE... BUT, IT'S HARD TO FEEL LIKE AN OUTSIDER.
I THINK THAT'S SOMETHING WE HAVE IN COMMON.

ALMOST AS LONELY AS YOUR CASTLE.
IT WASN'T ALWAYS LIKE THIS...
BELLE...
WHAT DO YOU SAY WE RUN AWAY?
WH...WHAT?

THE ENCHANTRESS GAVE ME THIS...
カチャ
ENCHANTRESS?
ANOTHER OF HER MANY CURSES.
SO THEY WERE CURSED BY SOMEONE...
HOW AMAZING!
A BOOK THAT TRULY ALLOWS YOU TO ESCAPE.

IT WAS HER CRUELEST TRICK OF ALL
THE OUTSIDE WORLD HAS NO PLACE FOR A MONSTER LIKE ME.
THINK OF THE PLACE YOU'VE MOST WANTED TO SEE.
THE PLACE I'VE...?
PAPA...
MOTHER...

WHERE DID YOU TAKE US?
PARIS.
THE PARIS OF MY CHILDHOOD...

OH, I LOVE PARIS.
WHAT WOULD YOU LIKE TO SEE FIRST?
NOTRE DAME? THE CHAMPS-ELYSEES?
I LEFT HERE A LONG TIME AGO, BUT MY FATHER NEVER DID.
HIS HEART HAS ALWAYS BEEN HERE, ALL MY LIFE...

ITS SO MUCH SMALLER THAN I IMAGINED...

I THOUGHT SEEING IT WOULD HELP ME UNDERSTAND...
BUT THERE'S NOTHING HERE.
THE CHILDHOOD I DREAMED OF... EXISTS ONLY IN MY MEMORIES.
WHAT HAPPENED TO YOUR MOTHER?

THAT'S THE ONLY STORY...
PAPA COULD NEVER BRING HIMSELF TO TELL ME.
ガ
チャ
THAT'S... !!

PLAGUE...
MY FATHER...
...WOULDN'T HAVE WANTED ME TO SEE THIS.

I AM SORRY
I EVER CALLED YOUR
FATHER A THIEF.
EVERYTHING HE'S DONE...
... WAS TO PROTECT ME.
BUT, STILL...

LET'S GO HOME.
...I'M GLAD TO KNOW THE TRUTH.

THANK YOU, CHIP!
WELCOME!
CHAPTER 6
HURRY UP NOW, DEAR.
MADAME ALMOST HAS YOUR DRESS READY!
I HOPE IT'S BETTER THAN THE LAST ONE...
EVERYTHING IS SO DIFFERENT...
EVEN IF I DO HAVE TO STAY HERE FOREVER... IT WOULDN'T BE SO BAD.

I HAVE FRIENDS HERE, AT LEAST...
ブクブクブクブク…
ドキドキ
ジャブ
チャポ…
BUT WHY AM I NERVOUS...?

THAT'S FOR ME?
OF COURSE, MY DEAR!
YOU LOOK BEAUTIFUL
THANK YOU...
GO ON, NOW... ENJOY YOUR DINNER.
I FEEL ANOTHER NAP COMING ON...

IT'S HARD TO BELIEVE THE CASTLE WAS SO DARK AND GLOOMY AT FIRST...

HE LOOKS SO REGAL...!

グイッ

I FEEL LIKE MY HEART'S GOING TO BURST...
HE LOOKS SO HAPPY...
AND MORE THAN THAT...
...HE LOOKS LIKE HE'S NEVER REALIZED HE COULD BE THIS HAPPY.

HE'S LESS SHY...
HE'S STANDING UP STRAIGHT... HE'S MORE ASSURED,
LESS WORRIED ABOUT HIS APPEARANCE...
I LIKE HIM BETTER THIS WAY. I LIKE HIM A LOT THIS WAY....
AND...I'M PROUD OF HIM.
HE HASN'T LOST HIS TEMPER IN DAYS... I THINK HE REALLY IS TRYING TO CHANGE.

I HAVEN'T DANCED IN YEARS. I'D ALMOST FORGOTTEN THE FEELING.
BELLE...
IT'S FOOLISH, I SUPPOSE...

...FOR A CREATURE LIKE ME TO HOPE THAT ONE DAY, HE MIGHT...
...EARN YOUR AFFECTION.

ドクン…
ドキ…
ドクン…
ドキ…
I DON'T KNOW...
REALLY? SO YOU THINK...
...YOU COULD BE HAPPY HERE?
I WOULDN'T HAVE THOUGHT SO AT FIRST. PERHAPS I COULD, BUT...
MY FATHER TAUGHT ME TO DANCE.
OUR HOUSE WAS ALWAYS FILLED WITH MUSIC...
CAN ANYONE BE HAPPY IF THEY AREN'T FREE?

COME WITH ME.
YOU MUST MISS HIM.
VERY MUCH.

GASP
PAPA!
WHAT ARE THEY DOING TO HIM?!

YOU MUST GO TO HIM.
WHAT...?
YOU ARE NO LONGER A PRISONER HERE.
NO TIME TO WASTE.
KEEP IT WITH YOU.
SO YOU WILL HAVE A WAY TO LOOK BACK ON ME.

THANK YOU.
THERE'S NOT ENOUGH TIME TO THANK YOU PROPERLY...
...BUT I PROMISE YOUR GENEROSITY WILL NOT BE FORGOTTEN.
I CANNOT SAY IF WE'LL EVER MEET AGAIN...
...BUT I WILL ALWAYS REMEMBER YOU AS MY FRIEND.

CHAPTER 7
STOP!
WHERE DID SHE COME FROM?
IS THAT BELLE?
LOOK AT THAT DRESS...

STOP THIS RIGHT NOW!
BELLE?
OPEN THIS DOOR! HE'S HURT.
I'M AFRAID WE CAN'T DO THAT, MISS...
...BUT WE'LL TAKE GOOD CARE OF HIM.
MY FATHER'S NOT CRAZY!
GASTON... TELL HIM!
BELLE, YOU KNOW HOW LOYAL I AM TO YOUR FAMILY...
...BUT YOUR FATHER HAS BEEN RAVING ABOUT A BEAST IN A CASTLE.

... AND THERE IS A BEAST.
OF COURSE...!

SHOW ME THE BEAST!

Well, it's hard to argue with that.

LOOK AT THIS BEAST.
LOOK AT HIS FANGS, HIS CLAWS!
THIS IS SORCERY!
NO, DON'T BE AFRAID! HE'S GENTLE AND KIND, AND...
オオオォ...

IF I DIDN'T KNOW BETTER, I'D SAY SHE EVEN CARED FOR THIS MONSTER!
SHE IS CLEARLY UNDER A SPELL!
HE'S NO MONSTER, GASTON.
THE BEAST WOULD NEVER HURT ANYONE!
YOU ARE!

THAT'S WHAT THEY SAID ABOUT THE PORTUGUESE MARAUDERS...
RIGHT BEFORE THEY SACKED AND PILLAGED HALF OF FRANCE!
!!
LOCK HER UP! HER FATHER, TOO!
DO YOU WANT TO BE NEXT?!
LEFOU, BRING ME MY HORSE!
!
GASTON, WITH ALL DUE RESPECT...

オオオオオ…
KILL THE BEAST!
ザッ…
ザッ…
ザッ…
GET HIM!
BELLE...
OH, PAPA I'M SO SORRY...!
I HAVE TO WARN HIM.
WARN HIM? HOW DID YOU GET AWAY FROM HIM?
I DON'T UNDERSTAND...
HE LET ME GO, PAPA! HE SENT ME BACK TO YOU.

HE TOOK ME TO MONTMARTRE.
BELLE, I HAD TO LEAVE YOUR MOTHER THERE...
I HAD NO CHOICE, I HAD TO SAVE YOU.
I KNOW, PAPA. I UNDERSTAND.

AND I HAVE TO SAVE HIM...
WILL YOU HELP ME?
BUT IT'S DANGEROUS.
YES. IT IS.
WE HAVE TO GET OUT OF HERE.
I COULD GET IT OPEN, IF I HAD SOMETHING TO PICK IT WITH...
SOMETHING LONG AND THIN, LIKE A...
...HAIR PIN!

I'M COMING BACK TO YOU...
PLEASE, JUST BE ALL RIGHT!
!!
ダッ
HE'S UPSTAIRS.

AND WHEN YOU SEE HIM...
...LET HIM KNOW THAT 'LE DUO' IS OVER!
I'M LE SINGLE NOW!
I HAVE MORE IMPORTANT WORDS FOR HIM THAN THAT...

WHAT HAVE YOU DONE?!
WHERE IS HE?!
YOU PREFER THAT MISSHAPEN MONSTER TO ME... WHEN I OFFERED YOU EVERYTHING?!
WHEN WE RETURN TO THE VILLAGE, YOU WILL MARRY ME
AND THE BEASTS HEAD WILL BE MOUNTED ON OUR WALL!

NEVER!

HE'S ALL RIGHT...!
!!
NO!

BELLE!
ザッ!!

WHAT CAN I DO?
I HAVE TO DO SOMETHING!
I HAVE TO SAVE HIM...!
GASTON, STOP!
!!

THIS IS HIS MOMENT...
...THIS IS HIS CHOICE, AND HIS CHANCE...
PLEASE...

I AM NOT A BEAST!
GO. GET OUT.

シュウウウ…
ジャリ…

YOU CAME BACK!
OF COURSE I CAME BACK!
I'LL NEVER LEAVE YOU AGAIN...
I'M AFRAID... IT'S MY TURN TO LEAVE.
AT LEAST I GOT TO SEE YOU AGAIN...
...ONE LAST TIME...
YOU CAN'T LEAVE ME NOW...
NO... PLEASE, NO...!
NOT WHEN I'VE FINALLY BEEN ABLE TO SEE YOUR GENEROSITY...

...YOUR COMPASSION, YOUR INTELLIGENCE... YOUR BRAVERY...
...NOT WHEN I'VE ONLY JUST REALIZED...
I LOVE YOU...!

WHAT...?!

BELLE...
IT'S ME!
ス…

...HE'S ALL RIGHT.

パァアア…アア
ギィイイ…
わっ

LOOK AT HIM...
SMILING, HAPPY...
EVERYONE IS SO GLAD TO SEE HIM, AND HE'S NOT AFRAID TO STAND AMONGST THEM.

I THINK WE'VE BOTH FOUND...
...HAPPILY EVER AFTER.

BELLE... WHAT ARE YOU THINKING?
EPILOGUE
WELL.. I WANT TO TURN THE LIBRARY INTO A SCHOOL
OF COURSE YOU DO.
AND OF COURSE YOU CAN. IT'S YOUR LIBRARY.

I WAS ALSO THINKING...
ABOUT "HAPPILY EVER AFTER".

IT'S HOW MY FAVORITE
STORIES ALWAYS ENDED...

...BUT THIS ISN'T AN END.

IT'S A BEGINNING.

"HAPPILY EVER AFTER"
IS A STORY, ITSELF.
ITS A CHOICE, EVERY DAY, TO BE
THE BEST PERSON YOU CAN BE.

TO TURN YOUR ANGER INTO PASSION......TO BRING CHANGE, NOT DESTRUCTION. TO FIND BEAUTY IN LOVE AND UNDERSTANDING...

...AND TO FIND "HOME"...

...WHEREVER YOU GO.

Disney
Beauty and the Beast
MANGA CONCEPT ART

It took many variations of rough concepts to find the best version that best captured the essence of the film character while maintaining a manga look and feel. Enjoy a few examples here!

BELLE Work-in-Progress
Sketches of Facial Expression

ベル
表紙すりよせ案
①

Manga Concept Sketches

YOUNG MAURICE'S HOUSE Freehand trace (for reference)

参考用〉

ヤングモーリス家
トレース・フリーハント

街並み
VILLENEUVE

BELLE'S BEDROOM in the Beast's Castle

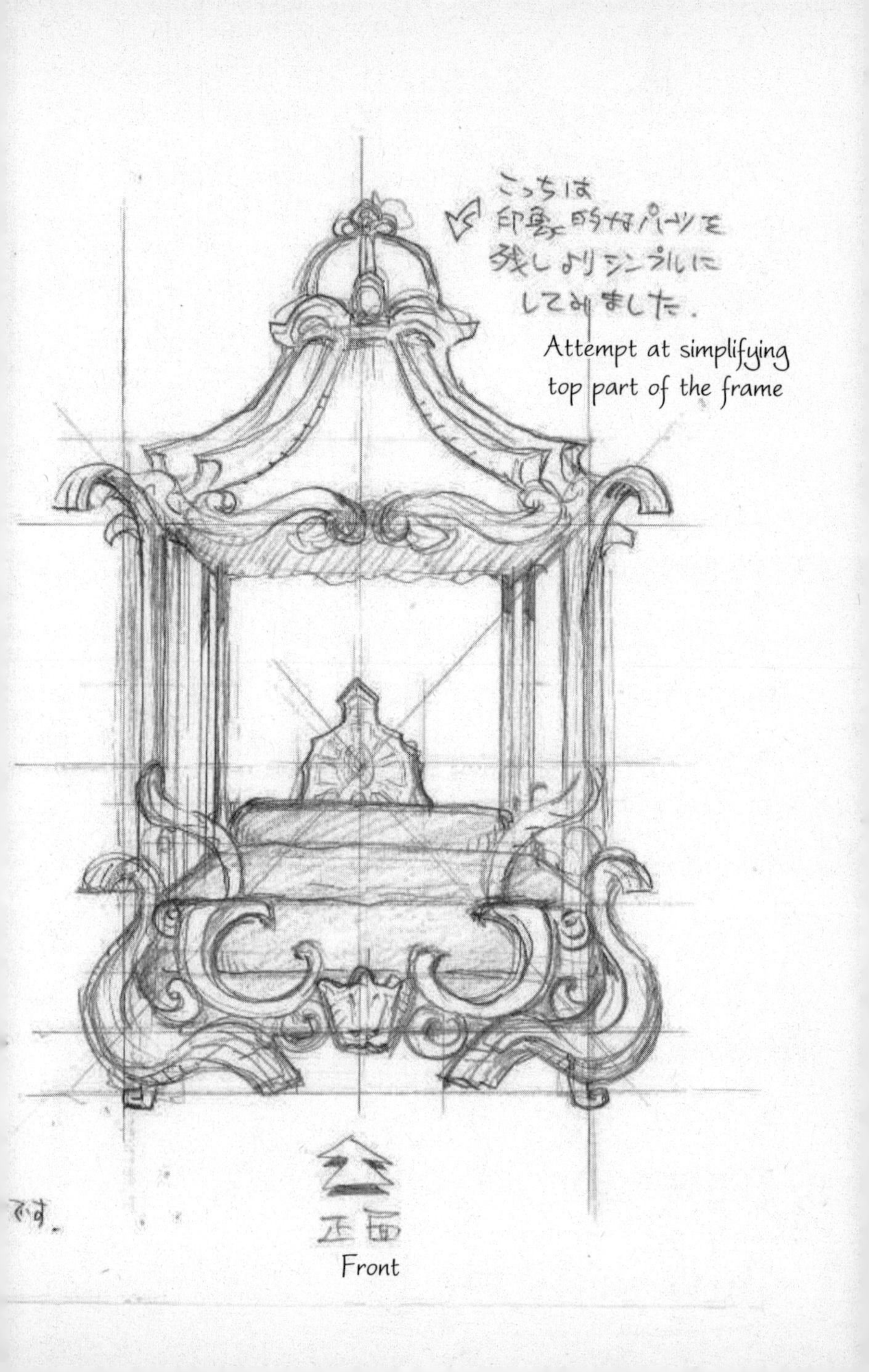
こっちは
印象的なパーツを
残しよりシンプルに
してみました。
Attempt at simplifying
top part of the frame
です。
正面
Front

ベルのベッド (ラフ画)
BELLE'S BED sketches
細かいディテールは
あいまい
きやらしくを優先
Details on
bed to match
overall style
水色部分は
布団(?)です
middle section
is the mattress
正面
Front
一応簡略化したつもりだ
まだシンプルにする必要
Front
Most likely need to
simplify this in the manga.

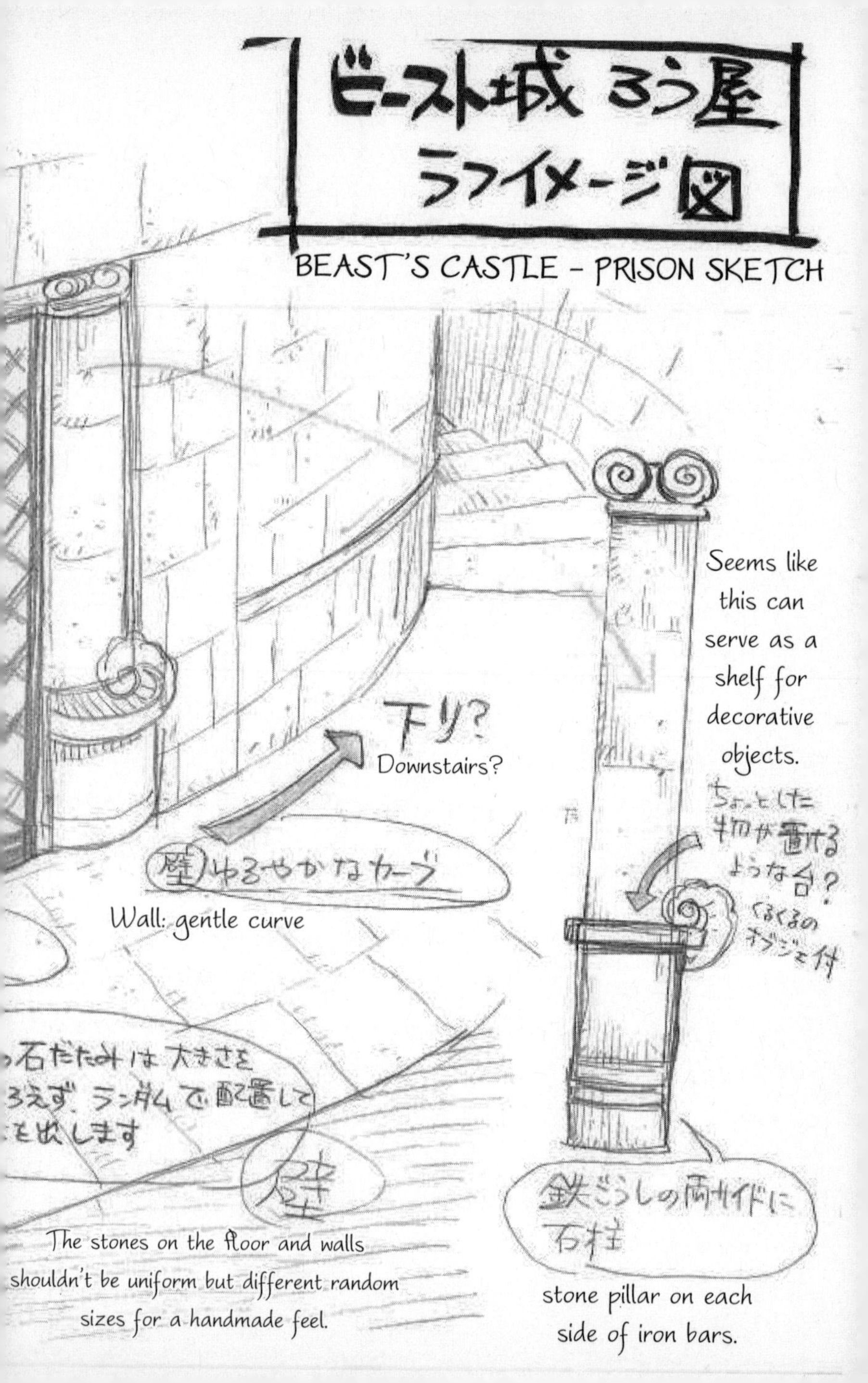

ビースト城 ろう屋
ラフイメージ図
BEAST'S CASTLE - PRISON SKETCH
下り？
Downstairs?
壁 ゆるやかなカーブ
Wall: gentle curve
Seems like this can serve as a shelf for decorative objects.
ちょっとした物が置けるような台？
くるくるのオブジェ付
石だたみは大きさを
ろえず ランダムで配置して
を出します
壁
The stones on the floor and walls shouldn't be uniform but different random sizes for a handmade feel.
鉄ごうしの両サイドに石柱
stone pillar on each side of iron bars.

Iron door – the main door opens with hinges; draw 2 long narrow lines on the side and 4 lines for the top.

アミアミ扉
開閉するメイン扉と
両サイドの細長い2枚
メイン扉の上に横長1枚
4枚を構成

Human size (Belle) approx?

人間サイズ(ベル)
このくらい?

Upstairs?

上り?

Door opens inwards

Hallway – not much room between the prison and wall, perhaps enough for 2 people to pass.

先に階段があって
予告でビーストが現れた
場所?

ろう下

ろう屋と壁面の幅は
そんなに広くはない
2人がすれ違える程度?

Stairs beyond here, perhaps where Beast appears in the movie trailer.

BEAST'S CASTLE - Library

ガストン
GASTON
新デザイン案
コミカルNG！
シリアスのみ！
New design, no comedic
just serious expressions!
コートのえり・そで
青エンピツ部分赤い
トーン処理
Collar and
cuffs use red
screentone
Gaston's ruffled
shirt – originally
thought by the artists
to be a scarf.
スカーフ？
構造が不明
衣装デザイン用のため
マンガ本編の等身とは
違います
Legs not drawn to scale – just
to emphasize costume design
ベルトバックル
belt buckle

STOP
THIS IS THE BACK OF THE BOOK!
How do you read manga-style? It's simple! To learn, just start in the top right panel and follow the numbers:
1
2
3
4
5
6
7
8
9
10

## *Disney Beauty and the Beast: Belle's Tale*

Art by: Studio Dice
Story Adapted by: Mallory Reaves

Publishing Assistant - Janae Young
Marketing Assistant - Kae Winters
Technology and Digital Media Assistant - Phillip Hong
Retouching and Lettering - Vibrraant Publishing Studio
Cover designer - Cody Matheson
Editor - Janae Young & Julie Taylor
Editor-in-Chief & Publisher - Stu Levy

Studio DICE

Hachi Mizuno
Pon Tachibana
Masashi Kuju
Rie Osanai
Kousuke Takezawa
Tatsuyuki Maeda
Sachika Aoyama
Eriko Terao
Shiori Soya
Takao Yabuno
Hisashi Nosaka

Concept Art by Hachi Mizuno
Cover Art by Hisashi Nosaka

Coordination by MITCHELL PRODUCTION, LLC
http://mitchellprod.com/en

TOKYOPOP Inc.
5200 W. Century Blvd. Suite 705
Los Angeles, 90045

E-mail: info@TOKYOPOP.com
Come visit us online at www.TOKYOPOP.com

www.facebook.com/TOKYOPOP
www.twitter.com/TOKYOPOP
www.youtube.com/TOKYOPOPTV
www.pinterest.com/TOKYOPOP
www.instagram.com/TOKYOPOP
TOKYOPOP.tumblr.com



ISBN: 978-1-4278-5683-8

First TOKYOPOP Printing: March 2017

10 9 8 7 6 5 4 3 2 1

Printed in the USA